MY PUPPY &
ME!
We love tennis!

WRITTEN BY
JANET FLEISHMAN

ILLUSTRATED BY
MARIA CORDREY

to:
_____

from:
_____

We practice tennis everyday.
I hit forehands and backhands...

It's so much fun to play!

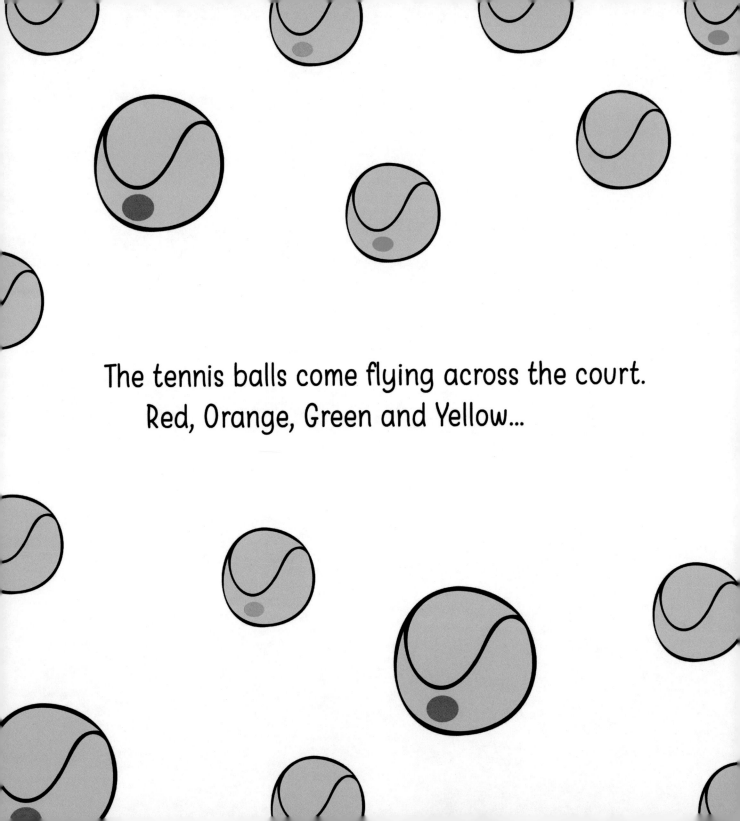

The tennis balls come flying across the court.
Red, Orange, Green and Yellow...

Tennis is definitely my **favorite sport!**

Oh NO!

My puppy stumbles and tumbles!
She's back on her paws...
She never even grumbles!

My favorite shot is the volley.
Short and simple...

Hey, there is
my tennis coach,
Molly!

It's time to hit some serves.
One, two, three, four...

Watch how much that
slice serve curves!

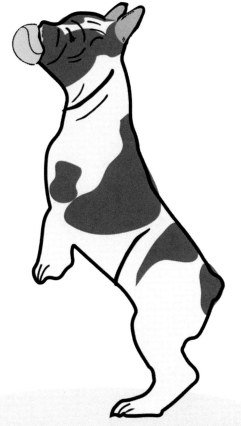

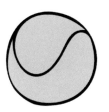

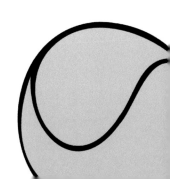

My puppy and I are getting faster
Focus, effort, hard work...
I want to be a tennis master!

My puppy and I make a great team.
A tennis championship...
Wow, would that be such a

dream!

Help us fill in these empty picture frames. Can you draw a picture of all your puppy adventures!

Can you help me decorate my dog collar?

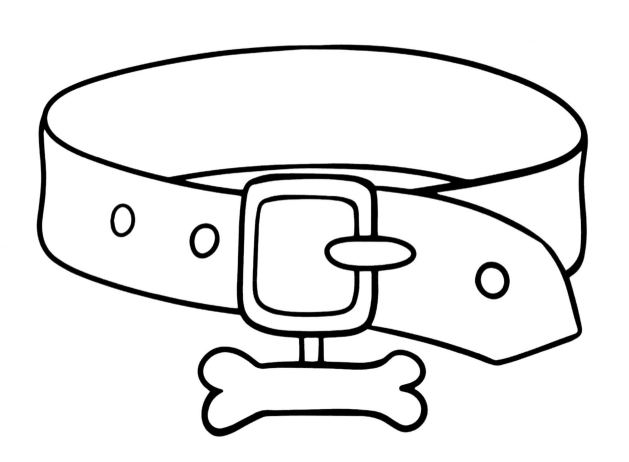

Check out all my books at
facebook.com/mypuppyandmelove